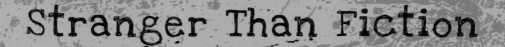

FAR-OUT FASHION

By Virginia Loh-Hagan

Disclaimer: This series focuses on the strangest of the strange. Have fun reading about strange people and things! But please do not try any of the antics in this book. Be safe and smart!

45th Parallel Press

Published in the United States of America by Cherry Lake Publishing
Ann Arbor, Michigan
www.cherrylakepublishing.com

Reading Adviser: Marla Conn MS, Ed., Literacy specialist, Read-Ability, Inc.

Photo Credits: © Studio KIWI/Shutterstock.com, cover; 24; © zentilla/Shutterstock.com, cover, 24; © OESIex/Shutterstock.com
1; © Belish/Shutterstock.com 5; © Kathy Hutchins/Shutterstock.com, 6; © Gonzales Photo/Alamy Stock Photo, 7; © OESIex/
Shutterstock.com 8; © Andre Luiz Moreira/Shutterstock.com, 9; © REDXIII/Shutterstock.com, 10; © South_agency/iStock.com, 12;
© Featureflash Photo Agency/Shutterstock.com, 13; © silentwings/Shutterstock.com, 14; © alexchern/Shutterstock.com, 15;
© Ttatty/Shutterstock.com, 16; © FashionStock.com / Shutterstock.com, 17; ©Tom Dorsey, Salina Journal/ASSOCIATED PRESS,
18; © Everett − Art/Shutterstock.com, 20; © julianne.hide/Shutterstock.com, 21; © ra3m/Shutterstock.com, 22 ; © VikaValter/
istock.com, 23; © Romaset/Shutterstock.com, 25; ©Margaret.W/Shutterstock.com, 26; © luanateutzi/Shutterstock.com, 27;
© Ollyy/Shutterstock.com, 27; © Matt Mohd/Shutterstock.com, 28; © Yu Zhang/Shutterstock.com, 29; © Alatom/iStock.com, 30

Graphic Element Credits: ©saki80/Shutterstock.com, back cover, front cover, multiple interior pages; ©queezz/Shutterstock.
com, back cover, front cover, multiple interior pages; ©Ursa Major/Shutterstock.com, front cover, multiple interior pages;
©Zilu8/Shutterstock.com, multiple interior pages

45th Parallel Press is an imprint of Cherry Lake Publishing.

Library of Congress Cataloging-in-Publication Data

Names: Loh-Hagan, Virginia, author.
Title: Far-Out fashion / by Virginia Loh-Hagan.
Description: Ann Arbor, Mich. : Cherry Lake Publishing, 2018. | Series:
   Stranger than fiction | Includes bibliographical references and index. |
   Audience: Grade 7 to 8.
Identifiers: LCCN 2018003310| ISBN 9781534129344 (hardcover) | ISBN
   9781534132542 (pbk.) | ISBN 9781534131040 (pdf) | ISBN 9781534134249
   (hosted ebook)
Subjects: LCSH: Fashion—Juvenile literature. | Body art—Juvenile literature.
Classification: LCC GT518 .L65 2018 | DDC 391—dc23
LC record available at https://lccn.loc.gov/2018003310

Printed in the United States of America
Corporate Graphics

About the Author

Dr. Virginia Loh-Hagan is an author, university professor, former classroom teacher, and curriculum designer. Her fashion consists of nightgowns and swimsuits. She lives in San Diego with her very tall husband and very naughty dogs. To learn more about her, visit www.virginialoh.com.

Table of Contents

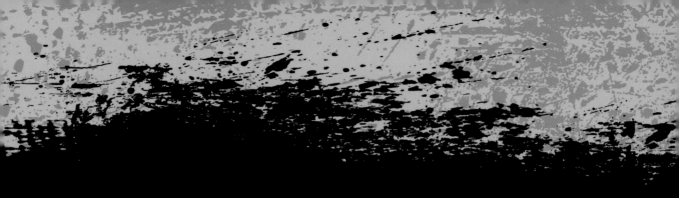

Introduction

Fashion is a style of dressing. It includes clothes. It includes shoes. It includes hair. It includes jewelry. It includes nails. People make fashion choices. They decide how they want to look. Some people set **trends**. Some follow trends. Trends are fads. They're what is popular at the time.

Fashion changes over time. It's different across cultures. It can be simple. It can be fancy. It can be crazy.

There's strange fashion. And then, there's really strange fashion. Some people make super strange fashion choices. They're so strange that they're hard to believe. They sound like fiction. But these stories are all true!

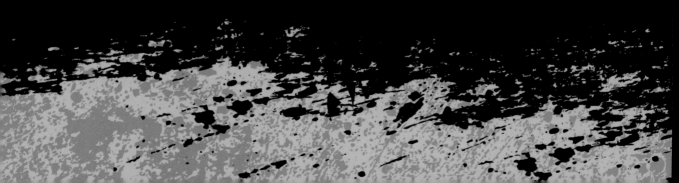

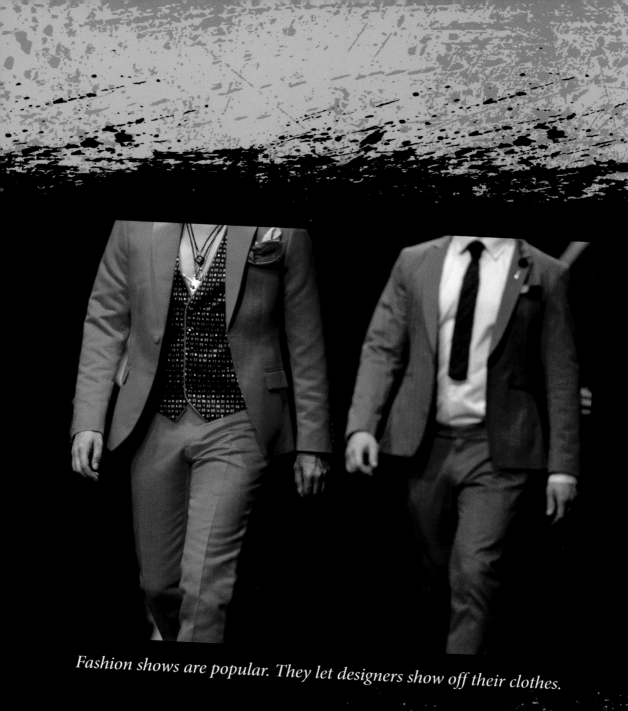

Fashion shows are popular. They let designers show off their clothes.

chapter one

Hammer Pants

Hammer pants were named for M. C. Hammer. Hammer was a rapper. He was famous in the 1980s and 1990s. He wore these pants in shows. He danced in them. He sang in them. He liked loose pants. He could do crazy dance moves. He said, "You move. And then the pants move. So it brings a nice little **flair**." Flair means style.

Hammer pants are baggy. They **billow** at the top. Billow means to expand. They sag in the middle. They **taper** at the ankle. Taper means to narrow. Hammer pants are colorful. They're shiny. They're flashy.

Hammer pants are inspired by pants worn in Iran, India, and Turkey.

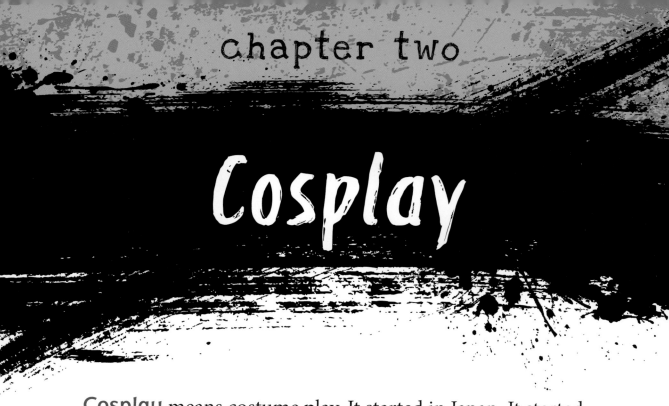

chapter two

Cosplay

Cosplay means costume play. It started in Japan. It started in 1984. It's a hobby. People wear costumes. They dress up like a favorite character. Characters come from movies. They come from cartoons. They come from video games. They come from comics. People can be anybody they want. They can make up their own characters. They can combine characters. There are no limits.

People also **role-play**. This means they act like the characters. They pretend. They make believe. They have big meetings.

People who cosplay are called cosplayers.

They dress up. They get together. The first World Cosplay **Summit** was in 2003. It took place in Japan. Summit means meeting.

Cosplay is a community. People become friends. They bond over their love of cosplay.

"Lolita," or "loli" for short, is a form of cosplay. It started in Japan. People dress in **Victorian** styles. Victorian is a time in history. Its fashion was more proper. It was during Queen Victoria's rule.

Lolita people wear big bows in their hair. They wear big dresses. They wear fancy material. They wear lace. They wear ruffles. They wear patterns. They wear lots of layers. They wear **petticoats**. Petticoats hang from the waist. They're like skirts worn under skirts.

People get together for "loli" events.

Explained
by Science

Fashion is all about colors. Color is a part of light. It's a moving wave. It travels over 186,000 miles (299,338 kilometers) per second. It affects people. Aristotle was an ancient Greek thinker. He said colors came from white and black. He related colors to water, air, earth, and fire. Then, Isaac Newton came up with another idea. Newton was a famous scientist. He saw light pass through a prism. He saw rainbow colors. The colors are the visible spectrum. Visible means being seen. Spectrum means a range. This rainbow spectrum is the bit of the light wave that we can see. Eyes have cones. Cones are special cells. They see these colors.

chapter three

Normcore

Normcore combines "normal" and "hard core." It's an **attitude**. Attitudes are how people think. It means finding freedom in being nothing special. It means acting basic. It's a trend. It started in 2014. It started as a joke. Young city people rebelled against being fancy. They became **anti**-fashion. Anti means against. Sean Monahan predicts trends. He said, "Normcore is a desire to be **blank**." Blank means not special.

People work hard to blend in. They wear useful clothes. They wear boring clothes. They wear regular clothes. They wear T-shirts. They wear sweatshirts. They wear jeans. They wear sneakers.

Selena Gomez is a good example of normcore.

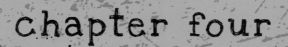

chapter four

Poison Dresses

"Poison green" dresses were popular in Victorian times. They cost a lot of money. They were bright green. They were made by using a lot of **arsenic**. Arsenic is an element. It's used as poison. People thought it was only bad if you ate it. It was used as a dye. It dyed **fabric**. Fabric is cloth. This dye was used to make dresses, gloves, shoes, and hair wreaths.

Women wore these things. They got sick. Their stomachs ached. They couldn't see. They got skin rashes. But they only wore these dresses for special events.

Arsenic was also connected to deep blue and red colors.

The people who made the dresses were at risk. They touched the dyes all the time. Some died.

chapter five

Tape

Tape art leaves people almost naked. It shows off the human body. People use tape. They cut it up into pieces. They cut it into shapes. They make patterns. They make designs. They create clothes using tape.

Joel Alvarez is a designer. He's from Miami. He started tape art. He calls it the Black Tape Project. He uses strong, black tape called electrical tape. Electrical tape is usually used for electrical wires. He takes 2 hours to decorate one body. He tapes up **models**. Models wear fashion. They help sell it. They go everywhere. They show off.

Alvarez is called the king of tape.

Duct tape is another type of tape. People make clothes made of duct tape. There's a duct tape fashion show. Many people participate. They show off what they made with duct tape. They wear shirts. They wear dresses. They wear pants. They wear duct tape jewelry.

The show takes place in Ohio. It's part of the Annual Duck Tape Festival. Duck Tape is a name of a company. It makes duct tape. In 2014, the show got a world record. There were 340 people dressed in duct tape. It was the most people in duct tape.

Some people even make duct tape boots!

Spotlight Biography

Alexander McQueen was a fashion designer. He was born in 1969. He died in 2010. He was known as the "bad boy wonder." He used strange objects in his fashion. He used bird feathers. He used crushed beetles. He used his own hair. He used antelope horns. He used worms. He once said, "I think there is beauty in everything." Tina Gorjanc loves McQueen's work. She's a fashion design student. She wants to make a special jacket. She wants to use McQueen's skin. She wants to use his cells. She'll grow his skin in a lab. She'll use McQueen's DNA. It will come from his hair. McQueen used his hair in one of his fashion designs. She wants to do this to prove a point. She wants people to stop killing animals.

chapter six

Black Teeth

Queen Elizabeth I was powerful. She was queen of England. She loved sugar. Sugar was special. Only rich people could eat sugar. Elizabeth ate a lot of sugar. Her teeth rotted. They smelled bad. They turned black. This sparked a trend. Women copied Elizabeth. They blackened their teeth. They wanted to prove they were rich, too.

The Japanese also blackened their teeth. This was called *ohaguro*. This means "blackened teeth." Women dyed their teeth. This meant they were rich. It meant they were grown up. The dye was made from iron and spices. It was helpful. It kept teeth healthy.

Some Japanese women still dye their teeth black.

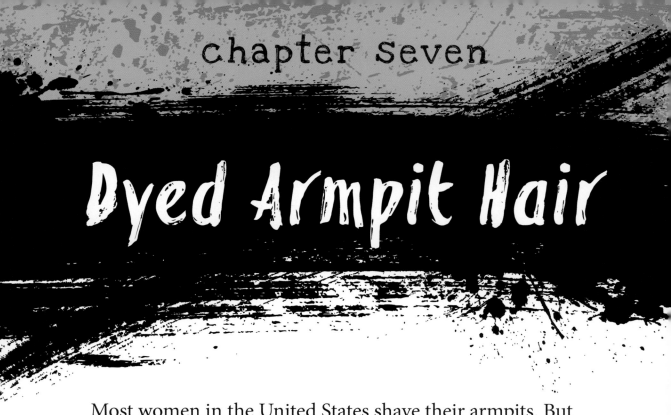

chapter seven

Dyed Armpit Hair

Most women in the United States shave their armpits. But some don't. They grow out their armpit hair. Some dye their armpit hair.

Roxie Hunt is a hairdresser. She's from Seattle. She dyed a woman's hair blue. Then she dyed her armpit hair blue. She said, "It was just sort of an **experiment**." Experiments are tests. She took photos. She shared them online. People liked this idea. They stopped shaving. They grew out their armpit hair. They started dyeing it. They dyed it different colors.

There's a movement called Free Your Pits.

Some women host "pit-ins." They get together. They dye their armpit hair.

chapter eight

Eyeball Jewelry

Eyeball jewelry started in the Netherlands. **Platinum** and gold are fancy metals. They're molded into different tiny shapes. Some shapes are hearts. Some shapes are stars. Some shapes are musical notes. Eye doctors put the platinum or gold pieces in the eye. They put it under the **cornea**. The cornea is the layer in front of the eye. Doctors make a tiny cut. They make a pocket. They place the metal in the pocket.

This process doesn't impact vision. People can still see. Other people can see the jewelry in their eyes. But U.S. doctors

Eyeball jewelry started in 2002.

think it's risky. They worry about blindness. They worry about eye sicknesses.

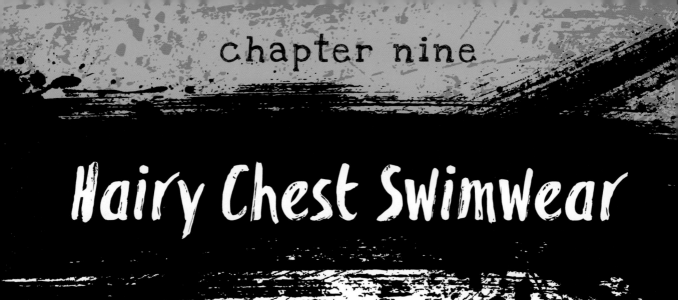

chapter nine

Hairy Chest Swimwear

Swimwear is clothes worn for swimming. It includes bikinis. It includes board shorts. Board shorts are shorts made for swimming.

Hairy chest swimwear is a real thing. It's a one-piece suit. It's usually worn by women. It has a picture of a man's hairy chest. It comes in different sizes. It comes in different skin tones. The tones are light, tan, or dark. The hair starts around the chest. It goes down to the **abs**. Abs are stomach muscles. The back is also hairy.

People can buy a full hairy body sweat suit. They can buy hairy chest T-shirts.

Hairy chest swimwear was created to shock people. They surprise people. They make people think. They give people something to talk about.

chapter ten

Lotus Shoes

Chinese girls used to bind their feet. This started as far back as 700 AD. It became a popular trend in the 12th century. It wasn't outlawed until 1912. Outlaw means to make illegal. Chinese people judged women by their foot size. Rich girls wanted small feet. They'd have better chances of getting married. Workers had normal feet. That's because they had to work. Over time, all girls were doing it. They wanted to copy rich people.

Girls soaked their feet in pee and vinegar. They broke their feet. They folded their feet over. They wrapped their feet. They

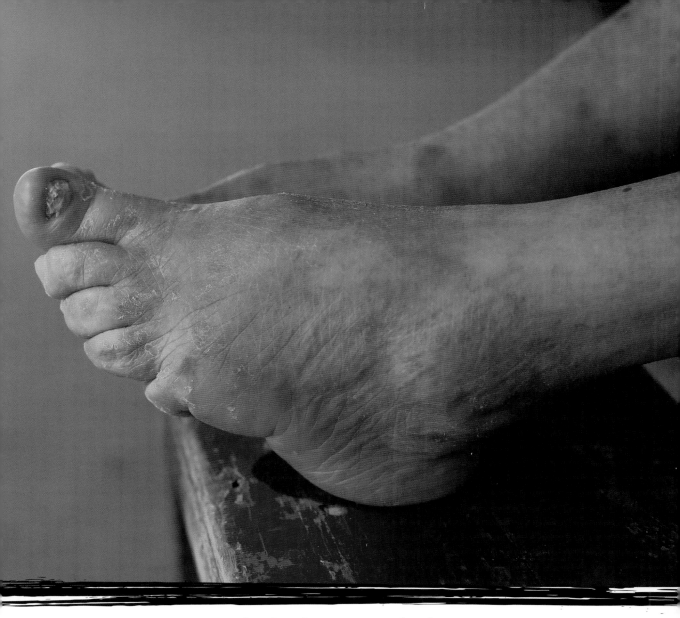

Foot-binding began in royal palaces.

used long ribbons. The ribbons stopped feet from growing. Some toes fell off. Girls kept breaking and folding their feet.

This process took several years. It was called **foot-binding**. Girls started at age 5. They wore **lotus** shoes. A lotus is a water lily. Lotus shoes were small. They fit in the palm of a hand. They were shaped like cones. They looked like lotus **buds**. Buds are plant sprouts. Lotus shoes were made of silk or cotton. They were colorful. They had fancy designs. The designs were flowers or animals.

Three-inch (7.6 centimeters) feet were called "golden lotuses." Four-inch (10 cm) feet were "silver lotuses." Five-inch (12.7 cm) feet were "iron lotuses."

Girls in lotus shoes walked like they were blowing in the wind.

Try This!

- Talk to people. Ask them how they choose their outfits.

- Research some fashion designers. Find out how they get their ideas.

- Design some clothes. Or put together outfits. Take pictures. Share with others.

- Watch videos about fashion shows. Get ideas. Then, host your own fashion show! Hire models to show off clothes.

- Make a fashion timeline. Pick a country. Pick three to five different time periods. Draw pictures of how people dressed. Include them on your timeline. Include captions. Compare past and present.

- Change your fashion style. Dress differently for a couple of days. See how people react to you.

Consider This!

Take a Position! Some people think fashion is art. Other people think fashion is distracting. They'd prefer uniforms. What do you think? For example, do you want a uniform policy at your school? Argue your point with reasons and evidence.

Say What? Think about your own fashion style. How would you describe it? What types of clothes do you like to wear? Think about what your friends wear. Explain how you are the same. Explain how you are different.

Think About It! Fashion has changed over time. Why do fashions change? Who sets fashion trends?

Learn More!

- Albee, Sarah. *Why'd They Wear That? Fashion as the Mirror of History*. Washington, DC: National Geographic, 2015.
- Black, Alexandra. *The Fashion Book*. New York: DK Publishing, 2014.
- Rubin, Susan Goldman. *Hot Pink: The Life and Fashions of Elsa Schiaparelli*. New York: Abrams Books for Young Readers, 2015.

Glossary

abs (ABZ) stomach muscles

anti- (AN-tye) against or opposed to

arsenic (AHR-suh-nik) element that could be used as poison

attitude (AT-ih-tood) way of thinking or feeling

billow (BIL-oh) to bulge

blank (BLANGK) not special, bland

buds (BUHDZ) plant sprouts

cornea (KOR-nee-uh) layer in the front of the eye

cosplay (KOS-play) costume play

experiment (ik-SPER-uh-ment) test

fabric (FAB-rik) cloth

fashion (FASH-uhn) style of dressing that includes clothes, shoes, hair, jewelry, and nails

flair (FLAIR) style, bling

foot-binding (FOOT-binde-ing) process of breaking and folding feet to make them smaller

lotus (LOH-tuhs) water lily

models (MAH-duhlz) people who wear fashion to try to sell it

petticoats (PET-ee-kohts) underskirts that hang from the waist

platinum (PLAT-uh-nuhm) fancy metal used in jewelry

role-play (ROHL-play) to act or pretend to be like someone else

summit (SUHM-it) meeting

swimwear (SWIM-wair) clothes worn for swimming

taper (TAY-per) to narrow down

trends (TRENDZ) fads or patterns

Victorian (vik-TOR-ee-uhn) of the time of Queen Victoria's reign

Index